# Magenta's Visit

**by Alice Wilder and Michael T. Smith**

**illustrated by Traci Paige Johnson and Karen Craig**

SCHOLASTIC INC.
New York   Toronto   London   Auckland   Sydney
Mexico City   New Delhi   Hong Kong

To my brother Lawrence, for being my friend forever—A. W.

To Shelley Hamm, who inspires me with her spirit and intelligence—M. T. S.

To Karen Cooper, my Magenta—T. P. J.

Special thanks to my grandfather, Sylvester S. Snyder, for all his wisdom, encouragement, and creative genes!—K. C.

## Note to Parents from Creators

As with all *Blue's Clues* books, *Magenta's Visit* was written based on the knowledge that preschoolers learn through everything they do. In exploring the theme of friendship with Blue, children will use thinking skills such as visual perception, associations, and problem solving. What does your child like to do when a friend comes over? Try the activities described in this book at their next play date!

Based on the TV series *Blue's Clues*® created by Traci Paige Johnson, Todd Kessler, and Angela C. Santomero as seen on Nick Jr.®
On *Blue's Clues*, Steve is played by Steven Burns.

ISBN 0-439-11415-2

12 11 10 9 8 7 6 5 4 3 2 1          9/9 0 1 2 3 4/0

Printed in the U.S.A.          24

First Scholastic printing, September 1999

Hi! It's me, Steve! We're so glad you're here today. Guess who else is here? It's someone special!

Magenta! Magenta is here! Hey, Magenta, what is your favorite
thing to do? Oh, we'll play Blue's favorite game Blue's Clues to
figure out what Magenta's favorite thing to do is.
Maybe Shovel and Pail want to play too. Let's go see.

You found everyone! Good job. Magenta, is hide-and-seek your favorite thing to do?

That's not your favorite? Wait a second . . .
did you find a clue? It's macaroni! Hmm. Maybe
Magenta's favorite thing to do is in the kitchen.
Let's look in there!

Mr. Salt and Mrs. Pepper are making animals out of food.

We made a turtle! Now let's make a pig and an ostrich. Which foods should we use?

Wow! Can you figure out how they made these animals?
Hey, Magenta, is this your favorite thing to do?

No, no, no.

What can it be? Oh, here's our second clue! It's a frame. Maybe Magenta's favorite thing to do is in the living room. Come on!

Great costumes! Magenta, is playing dress-up your favorite thing to do?

Hey, look at all these pictures. Let's see where they're coming from.

Tickety, were you taking pictures?

Oh, that's what those pictures are. It looks like you got a little too close, Tickety. Magenta, is taking pictures your favorite thing to do?

No . . . oh, wait! Here's our third clue. It's glue. We have
all three clues!  Now where do we go?

The Thinking Chair! Now that we're in our thinking chair, let's think. The clues are macaroni, a picture frame, and glue.

Hmm . . . now do you know what Magenta's favorite thing to do is?

Making macaroni picture frames! That's Magenta's favorite thing to do. You figured out Blue's Clues. You are so smart!